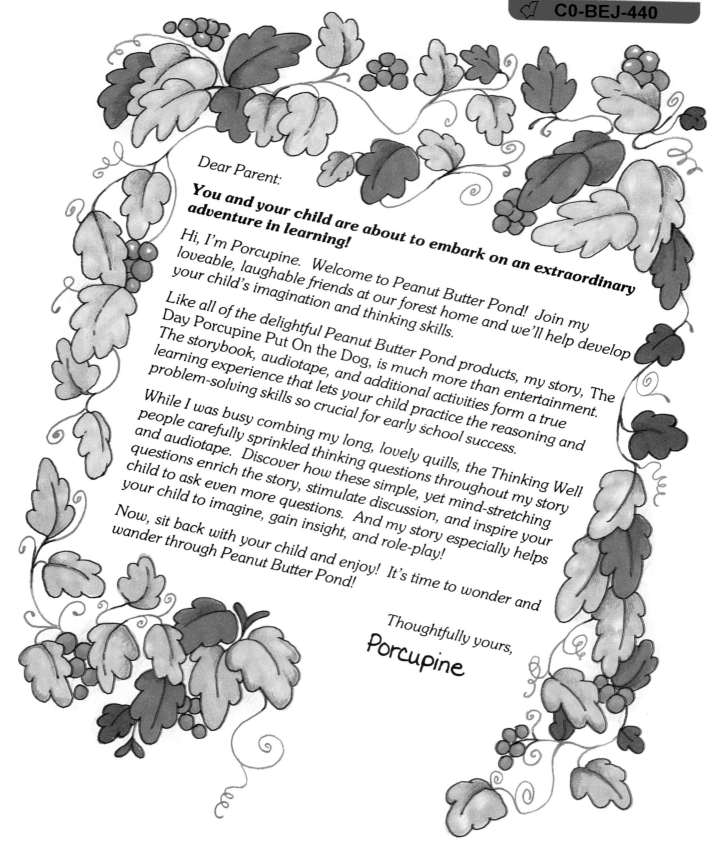

Dear Parent:

You and your child are about to embark on an extraordinary adventure in learning!

Hi, I'm Porcupine. Welcome to Peanut Butter Pond! Join my loveable, laughable friends at our forest home and we'll help develop your child's imagination and thinking skills.

Like all of the delightful Peanut Butter Pond products, my story, The Day Porcupine Put On the Dog, is much more than entertainment. The storybook, audiotape, and additional activities form a true learning experience that lets your child practice the reasoning and problem-solving skills so crucial for early school success.

While I was busy combing my long, lovely quills, the Thinking Well people carefully sprinkled thinking questions throughout my story and audiotape. Discover how these simple, yet mind-stretching questions enrich the story, stimulate discussion, and inspire your child to ask even more questions. And my story especially helps your child to imagine, gain insight, and role-play!

Now, sit back with your child and enjoy! It's time to wonder and wander through Peanut Butter Pond!

Thoughtfully yours,

Porcupine

ISBN 1-55999-123-2

A division of LinguiSystems, Inc.

Thinking Well
3100 4th Avenue
East Moline, IL 61244

1-800-U-2-THINK

The Day Porcupine
Put On the Dog
at Peanut Butter Pond

Story by Lael Littke
Illustrated by Stephanie McFetridge Britt

One morning, Porcupine looked into the clear waters of Peanut Butter Pond and saw her reflection.

She saw her tiny, little eyes and pug, little nose. She saw her pudgy, round body, bristling with quills. She saw her small, stubby tail.

"I'm ugly," she said. "I must be the ugliest one around here."

Skunk and Snake and Bird came to look.

"You aren't so bad, Porcupine," Skunk said. "Lots of animals are uglier than you."

Porcupine looked hopeful. "Really? Which ones?"

Skunk thought for a long time. "I can't think of one right now," he said.

Why does Porcupine think she is ugly?

"But don't worry, Porcupine," Skunk said. "It isn't all that important to be beautiful." He looked at his own reflection in Peanut Butter Pond and combed his claws through his glossy black-and-white fur.

Bird ruffled his bright blue feathers.
        "If you ask my advice,
            it's more important to be nice."
Bird was studying to be a poet. As he flew away, he added,
        "Of course it's best if you can be
            both beautiful and nice — like me!"

Porcupine sighed mournfully. "I'm tired of being ugly. I'm going to do something about it."

What do you think Porcupine is going to do?

Porcupine went into her house and got out her mail-order catalog.
On page 16, she found just what she wanted.

She wrote out an order, enclosed a check, addressed an envelope, and gave it to Mail Mouse.

What will Mail Mouse do with the envelope?

While she waited for her order to come, Porcupine went to Peanut Butter Pond General Store.

She bought false eyelashes to make her eyes look larger. She bought red fingernail polish to put on her claws. She bought lipstick and blush and Evening in the Swamp perfume.

Let's pretend we're smelling Porcupine's new perfume. How does it smell?

A week later, Mail Mouse brought what Porcupine had ordered. As he handed the package to her, he said, "I met Dawg over by Thorn Bush. He was headed this way."

Dawg lived at Nearby Farm, behind a fence with a sign that said

But Porcupine wasn't worried. Dawg was only dangerous when he'd been fighting with Poodle, who lived next door.

"I'll watch for him," Porcupine said as Mail Mouse left.

BEWARE
OF
DAWG

Skunk and Bird and Snake came to see what Porcupine
had ordered from her catalog.

Porcupine opened the package and took out what was inside.

What do you think is inside the package?

Porcupine held it up. It was curly and blonde.

Bird flapped his wings and chirped,
        "Why, it's a wig,
        but it's too big!"

Porcupine shook her head. "No, it isn't. Wait and see!"

Why did Bird think the wig was too big?

Porcupine went into her house and put on her new eyelashes and fingernail polish. She put the lipstick and blush on her face, and dabbed some perfume behind her ears.

Then she put on the curly, blonde wig. She put it on her whole body, from her head to her tail. It covered up all of her quills.

"It's just right!" Porcupine exclaimed.

How does Porcupine feel now?

Porcupine went outside to show the others.

"TA-DA!" Porcupine said, announcing herself.

They all gasped when they saw her.

Bird looked at Porcupine and twittered,
        "Can it be true
            that this is you?"

"No," said Porcupine. "It's not me anymore. I'm a new animal.
Call me Muriel."

Snake stood right up on his tail to admire her.
"You're sssso very beautiful, Muriel."

What's another name Porcupine could call herself?

Porcupine gazed at her new reflection in Peanut Butter Pond.
"Yes, I am!" She fluffed up her curly, blonde hair.

Just then, Dawg came ambling into the clearing. He squinted as he looked around. Dawg was very nearsighted.

"Rowr, rowr, rowr!" he barked.

"Ssssay, he's in a bad mood," Snake hissed as he slithered under a log.

"Dawg must have been fighting with Poodle," Skunk whispered as he ran into the forest to hide.

Bird flew to the top of Tall Tree.

Porcupine tried to run and hide, too, but she could barely move because the body wig got in her way.

What would you do if you were Porcupine? Why?

Suddenly, Dawg stiffened. He stared at Porcupine through his weak eyes. He walked toward her. The fur around his shoulders stood up angrily. He sniffed at Porcupine.

"Aha!" he said. "It's Poodle!"

"I'm not Poodle!" Porcupine announced. "I'm Muriel."

Dawg put his nose close to Porcupine. "Poodle has curly, blonde fur. Poodle always smells like a perfume store. You *have* to be Poodle!"

What could Porcupine do so Dawg knows it's really her?

Dawg opened his mouth wide. Porcupine could see his shiny, white teeth.

Porcupine tried to put up her quills, but she couldn't because of the wig. She tried to close her eyes, but her long eyelashes were tangled in her curly, blonde hair.

Why did Porcupine want to close her eyes?

Dawg's jaws snapped shut, right on Porcupine's wig.

The wig came off in his mouth!

Dawg shook it.

He chewed on it.

He gnarled it.

The wig began to come apart!

Should Porcupine try to stop Dawg from tearing her wig?

Hairs from the wig stuck to Dawg's tongue. "P-too!" he said, dropping what was left of the wig.

Now that Porcupine's quills were uncovered, she could make them stand up. She rattled them loudly. If Dawg tried to bite her, she'd fill his nose full of needles!

Dawg stared at Porcupine. He looked very confused.

"Porcupine, where did you come from?" he asked. Then he pawed at his mouth. "P-too! Poodle's fur came off in my mouth. She won't be so stuck-up now that she's bald!"

Porcupine picked up what was left of the wig. "You'd better take Poodle's fur back to her before she catches cold, Dawg."

"No way," Dawg said. "She can come get it herself. P-too!"

Is Porcupine still in danger? Why or why not?

Dawg turned and ambled back into the forest. Porcupine could hear him saying "P-too! P-too!" until he was out of sight.

As soon as Dawg was gone, Skunk crept into the clearing. Bird fluttered down from Tall Tree, and Snake slithered out of his hiding place under the log.

"You're very nice to save us all, Muriel," Skunk said. "But, it's too bad Dawg ruined your wig."

"I don't care," Porcupine said. "I'm taking Bird's advice. It's more important to be nice."

Snake stood up on his tail to gaze at her. "You *are* beautiful, Muriel."

Porcupine smiled. "Please, call me Porcupine," she said.

Think 'n' Tell

Tell me about someone who is nice to you. What makes that person so nice?

Pretend Porcupine received a pair of scissors instead of a wig. Draw a picture of how Porcupine might look.

How is a catalog like a store? How is it different?

What are some ways you try to make yourself look nice?

Bird talks in rhyme. Make up a rhyme that Bird might say when he is hungry, cold, or tired.

Dawg!

Dawg is really a friendly animal. Make your own cup Dawg and see for yourself. Take him for a walk, but keep him away from Poodle!

What you need:

glue	2 paper cups
scissors	white paper
yarn	construction paper
pencil	

What to do:

1. Put one cup upside down on a sheet of paper. Draw a circle around the edge of the cup. Then, move the cup and draw another circle around the edge. Cut out both circles.

2. Glue one circle over the top of one cup. Glue the second circle over the top of the other cup.

3. Turn one cup upside down on the table to make Dawg's body.

4. Turn the other cup on its side. Glue it on top of the cup that is upside down to make Dawg's head.

5. Draw two large ears, two eyes, a nose, a tongue, and a collar on construction paper. Cut out each piece. Glue each piece on Dawg.

6. Cut a piece of yarn. Glue it to Dawg's collar for a leash.

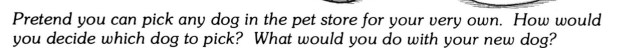

Pretend you can pick any dog in the pet store for your very own. How would you decide which dog to pick? What would you do with your new dog?

You're Beautiful, Porcupine!

Porcupine's friends know she is beautiful. Make a poster for Porcupine to show her how beautiful you think she is.

What you need:

crayons	toothpicks
glue	construction paper

What to do:

1. Write the word *I* on one side of your paper.

2. Draw a heart in the middle.

3. Draw a picture of Porcupine on the other side.

4. Glue quills (toothpicks) on Porcupine.

5. Write your name at the bottom of the page.

Ask all your friends who think Porcupine is beautiful to write their names on your poster, too. Tape your poster to a window. Now, if Porcupine walks by, she can see how many people love her, just the way she is.

Pretend you are Porcupine. How would you feel if you saw this poster taped on a window?

Porcupine Makes Waiting Fun!

Porcupine had to wait many days before Mail Mouse delivered her new wig. Sometimes waiting for something special is hard to do! Make a Porcupine calendar and make your waiting fun!

What you need: potato   4 buttons
                     toothpicks

What to do:

1. Count the number of days until the next holiday or special event you are waiting for.

2. Count out the same number of toothpicks. Push each toothpoick into the top or sides of the potato. The toothpicks are now Porcupine's quills!

3. Give Porcupine a button face. Break 2 toothpicks in half. Push a toothpick halfway into the potato where the eyes, nose, and mouth will be. Hang the buttons on the toothpicks.

Put Porcupine close to your bed. Then, watch the days disappear as you pull one toothpick out of your Porcupine calendar each night.

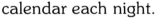

What special day are you waiting for? Why?
Have fun looking forward to your special day!

Just Being Me!

Early one morning, by Peanut Butter Pond,
Porcupine looked very sad. We asked her what was wrong.
"I'm so unhappy about my stubby tail.
I'll order all the things I need and get them in the mail."

CHORUS

But Porcupine found out one day that looks don't count at all.
It's really how you treat your friends that matters, after all.
"Now I'm so happy, just being me.
Being nice to friends is the key."

Porcupine, you're happy!
We'll always be your friends.
We think the way you are is fine!
We'll love you to the end!